Unicorn Stories

The Singing Unicorn

Jan Rylewicz

Om KIDZ
An imprint of Om Books International

AF516737

The sky opera stood in the clouds above the mountains.

It showed unicorn dances, unicorn cinema and unicorn sports like horn-locking and eyelash-fluttering.

But it was mainly used for sky operas. Only unicorns were allowed in it.

Madame Anya was the diva at the opera, singing almost every night.

"La la la la la," she neighed, so shrill that the moon and the sun moved out of position.

All the unicorns applauded with clacking hooves.

Another great performance!

One day, the unicorn singer, Calypso, challenged Madame Anya. Calypso and her daughter Gal were from the poor part of the forest.

Gal wanted her mother to win the first prize. The family badly needed money for food.

The night of the singing duel in the sky opera had come.

"I brought popcorn!" said Godfrey, Gal's younger brother. But as he said it, half of the packet spilled into his lap. "Oh, no!"

"Are you nervous, mother?" asked Gal.

Her mother had never looked prettier. She had even highlighted her hair, the yellow of the evening stars.

"Unicorns don't get nervous!" she lied.

Madame Anya stepped on the stage. She wore a silken throw and a diamond tiara. The crowd cheered.

She opened the competition.

She sang, as if opening her mouth for a doctor.

"What is she doing now?" asked Godfrey.

"She is tuning," explained Gal.

Madame Anya's mouth was open so wide that stars bounced from it, sparkling in the night sky. Every high note turned into a baby star, and every low one into a purple planet.

At the end of her performance, the night sky was full of new lights. The wild applause lasted almost all night.

But Madame Anya was jealous. She did not want her challenger to win!

Calypso came on the stage, and Gal cheered loudly. Only tired Godfrey had fallen asleep inside his popcorn.

Calypso opened her mouth, and raised her horn to the stars. She began to sing beautifully.

“IIIIIIIIIIIIIIIIIIIIIIIIIIIIIIIIIII
WIIIIIIIIIIIIILLLLLLLLLLLLLLLL
ALWAAAAAAAAAAAAAAAAAYS LOOOVE….”

But, a jealous Madame Anya secretly tripped her up. And nobody saw her do it!

Calypso fell through the cracks in the clouds and sailed through the sky, landing roughly on the top of a willow tree.

She was injured, and was not able to sing again.

Gal was very sad.

"How will we make money? What will we eat?" she worried.

One day, Gal read the following headline in the newspaper:

PALACE PALLADIUM OPENS DOORS TO STUDENTS.

It was a new singing school, and the main teacher was Madame Anya.

Gal was angry. She decided to sing at the new school and to get the diva arrested!

Gal and Godfrey ate the same meal every day. Cold stinging nettles for breakfast, and steamed stinging nettles for lunch and dinner. Something had to change.

The next morning, Gal set out before the break of dawn. As she flew deeper into the forest, she met other animals, who wanted to sing at the Palace Palladium.

There was Mayhem, the monkey, who was good at rapping.

Lotus, the Japanese salamander, who was good on the recorder.

There was the locust brass section, a mini orchestra from Africa.

Freddy Flea, a microscopic singer, yet a superstar amongst the little people.

Benji, the elephant, a master on the trombone, who could carry a dog or a cat on the air he blew out of his trunk.

Hector, the lion, was a rock drummer with a big beard.

When they reached the brand new school, the animals were nervous. They were scratching their heads and shaking their hooves, stinging with their stingers and striking with their tails.

Not a single one of them stood still.

Angry Madame Anya opened the balcony windows and shouted:

"Stop fidgeting. Anyone who doesn't stand still in ten seconds is disqualified!"

Freddy, the flea, was the first contestant. Yet he was so small that Madame Anya didn't even hear him!

He was sad when he left the hall.

Next up was Hector, the lion, who beat his drums hard like thunder with his paws and tail.

"Far too loud!" complained the diva and kicked him out. Hector looked angry.

Now it was Mayhem monkey's turn. He cleared his throat and got ready to rap. But he couldn't.

What if she didn't like rap?

"What is it?" asked the impatient diva.

"Just a second," screeched Mayhem.

"Get out. There is no room in this school for stage fright!" yelled the ugly diva, and kicked Mayhem out.

Gal gave him a big hug.

"Don't worry, it will all be fine," she said.

Gal stormed into the hall. Madame Anya leaned lazily on a cushion, drinking sweet unicorn chocolate milk.

"You pushed my mother down the sky opera because you knew she was a better singer than you!"

Madame Anya laughed loudly.

"Of course! I pushed her! I am the only unicorn superstar. Nobody is allowed to challenge me."

But clever Gal recorded the diva's confession. Soon, the unicorn police arrived to arrest her.

By now, Calypso had recovered from her fall. She became the new singing teacher at the Palace Palladium. Everyone loved her.

Gal often sang duets with her mother. Now, the family had enough food and money to live.

Mayhem monkey passed all his rap exams and made everyone proud.